The Fossil Hunters

Marilyn Helmer

illustrated by **Dermot Walshe**

ORCA BOOK PUBLISHERS

For my good friend Judith,
and especially for Lily and Sophie.

Library and Archives Canada Cataloguing in Publication

Helmer, Marilyn
The fossil hunters / Marilyn Helmer ; illustrated by Dermot Walshe.

(Orca echoes)
ISBN 978-1-55469-191-3

I.†Walshe, Dermot, 1962- II. Title. III.†Series:†Orca echoes

PS8565.E4594F68 2009   jC813'.54   C2009-904579-6

First published in the United States, 2009
Library of Congress Control Number: 2009932876

Summary: Shelley feels left out when she visits her cousin Kyle at his lakeside cottage
and finds that his friend Marcus is staying there too.

Orca Book Publishers gratefully acknowledges the support for its publishing programs
provided by the following agencies: the Government of Canada through the Book
Publishing Industry Development Program and the Canada Council for the Arts, and the
Province of British Columbia through the BC Arts Council
and the Book Publishing Tax Credit.

Cover artwork and interior illustrations by Dermot Walshe

Orca Book Publishers
PO Box 5626, Stn. B
Victoria, BC Canada
V8R 6S4

Orca Book Publishers
PO Box 468
Custer, WA USA
98240-0468

www.orcabook.com
Printed and bound in Canada.
12 11 10 09 • 4 3 2 1

Chapter One
WHERE IS KYLE?

Shelley couldn't sit still. "How much longer until we get there?" she asked.

"That's the twenty-hundredth time you've asked," said Dad.

Shelley giggled. "Dad, there's no such number as twenty-hundredth," she said.

"We'll be there soon," said Mom.

Shelley sighed. "Soon" was taking much too long. She couldn't wait to get to Gray Rocks Lake and see Aunt Joan and Uncle Ray. And Topper. But most of all, she couldn't wait to see her cousin Kyle.

Last summer, Shelley and Kyle went swimming, hiking, paddleboating and picnicking. They built forts and made a tree house and played explorers. They even had their own special club. It was called The Beach Club. Shelley had thought up the name because the beach was their favorite place to play.

"Look, Shelley," said Mom. She pointed to a sign on the road.

"Gray Rocks Lake," Shelley cheered. "Yay! We're almost there."

A few minutes later, Dad turned onto a grassy driveway. Shelley scrambled out of the car. "We're here!" she shouted.

The screen door flew open, and Uncle Ray and Aunt Joan rushed out.

Everyone hugged and kissed. But where was Kyle? I'll bet he's hiding until the hugging and kissing is over, thought Shelley.

A friendly brown dog ran out of the bushes.

"Topper!" cried Shelley. Topper wiggled and wagged. She dropped a rubber ball at Shelley's feet. The ball had once been white. Now it was gray.

It was lumpy and lopsided. She barked for Shelley to throw the ball.

Shelley picked up the ball and threw it across the grass. Topper raced after it.

"She's happy to see you," said Aunt Joan. "She misses Kyle."

Misses Kyle? Shelley's heart sank. Where was Kyle?

Chapter Two
ANOTHER GUEST

"Kyle has been away all week at his friend's cottage," said Aunt Joan.

"He'll be back this afternoon," said Uncle Ray.

Shelley breathed a huge sigh of relief. Spending a whole week with only adults for company wasn't what she had been expecting.

Dad and Uncle Ray went to get the luggage. Mom and Aunt Joan went inside. Shelley stayed outside to play with Topper.

After a while, Shelley's arm got sore. She sat down at the picnic table. "I'm sorry, Topper," she said. "I'm too tired to play ball anymore."

Topper lay down at Shelley's feet. She put her head between her paws.

"I'll play with you again later," said Shelley.

A car turned onto the driveway. Topper's ears perked up. She scrambled to her feet and grabbed her ball.

The car door swung open, and Kyle jumped out. He had a big smile on his face.

Shelley ran to meet him. She felt happy all the way to her fingertips. We're going to have so much fun together! she thought.

Then, to Shelley's surprise, another boy stepped out of the car. He stared at Shelley. He was not smiling.

"Marcus, come meet my cousin Shelley," Kyle called.

Marcus walked over slowly. "Hi," he muttered. He looked at Shelley. "How old are you?"

"I'm eight," said Shelley.

"I'm ten," said Marcus. "You're just a kid."

"I am not a kid," Shelley declared. She decided she did not like Marcus very much. She wished he would get back in his car and go home.

A woman got out of the car too. She took a suitcase from the trunk. "Kyle, come and get your suitcase," she called.

"I'll be back in a minute," Kyle said to Shelley.

The screen door opened. Aunt Joan came out. "Hi, Beth," she called. "Will you come in for a cup of tea?"

The woman shook her head. "Thanks, Joan, but I have to get back," she said. "We have company coming tonight."

Shelley almost cheered out loud. Yay! Marcus would be going home now.

Marcus's mom reached into the trunk again. She took out another suitcase. She gave it to Marcus. "Have fun," she said. "I'll be back to pick you up at the end of the week."

Shelley almost groaned out loud. Marcus was staying for the whole week?

"These three are going to have a great time together," said Aunt Joan.

Marcus scowled at Shelley. Shelley scowled back. Something told her this week was going to be anything but fun.

Chapter Three
A RAINY DAY

Dad knocked on the bedroom door. "Come on, Sleepyhead," he called. "Everyone else is up already."

Shelley yawned. She felt tired and grumpy. Kyle and Marcus had kept her awake last night, giggling and talking in the next room.

"Last call to breakfast," Uncle Ray shouted from the kitchen.

"Better hurry," said Dad.

Shelley rolled out of bed. She looked out the window. Oh no! Rain pelted against the glass. That meant no swimming, boating, hiking or picnicking. It meant no exploring or building forts and clubhouses. It meant an indoor day.

Shelley remembered a rainy day last summer. They'd had a Monopoly tournament. Everyone joined in. They made popcorn. They toasted marshmallows and made s'mores in the fireplace. A rainy day could be a fun day too. Shelley didn't feel tired or grumpy anymore.

After breakfast, Shelley helped with the dishes. Topper came into the kitchen. She had her old gray ball. She went to the door and looked back at Shelley. Topper wanted to play outside.

Shelley scratched Topper's ears. "I'll play fetch with you when it stops raining," she said. "Right now I'm going to get everyone to play Monopoly."

Shelley went looking for Kyle. He and Marcus were in the living room. Cardboard boxes and pieces of wood littered the floor.

Kyle looked up. "We're making a city," he said. "It's going to be huge. Do you want to help?"

"There isn't room for three people to work on it," said Marcus.

"Sure there is," said Kyle. He pushed aside markers and scissors and scraps to make room for Shelley.

Shelley picked up a tall box. "I can make a neat apartment building with this," she said.

"You can't use that," said Marcus. "It's part of my garage."

"Here, Shelley," said Kyle. He held out a piece of cardboard. "You can make the road signs for our city."

"I don't want to make road signs," said Shelley. "Let's play Monopoly instead."

Chapter Four
LEFT OUT

"Kyle and I are too busy to play kid's games," said Marcus.

"Monopoly is not a kid's game," Shelley declared. "Last summer everyone played."

"So go play with everyone else," said Marcus. "Kyle and I are busy."

Shelley was mad and sad. Marcus was the meanest person she had ever met. She felt like stomping on his garage.

"We can all play together as soon as Marcus and I finish our city," said Kyle.

Everyone else was busy too. Uncle Ray was working at his computer. Dad was sorting his fishing gear.

Mom and Aunt Joan had gone into town. There was no one to play Monopoly with.

Shelley went out to the porch. The rain had stopped. She felt a thump against her leg. Topper looked up at her.

"Do you want to play with me?" Shelley asked.

As soon as Topper heard the word "play," her tail whipped back and forth in delight. Then she stuck her head under the table and grabbed her ball.

"Let's go play fetch," said Shelley. Topper followed her outside.

A while later, Kyle and Marcus came out. They joined in the game too.

Topper yelped with excitement. Now she had three people to play fetch with.

It was Shelley's turn to throw the ball. Topper caught it before it hit the ground.

"You have to throw harder," said Marcus. "Watch this." He threw Topper's ball. The ball flew far into the bushes. Topper raced after it.

A car door closed. Shelley's mom and Aunt Joan were back from town. "We stopped at the deli," Mom said. "Come and have some lunch."

By the time they finished eating, the sun was out. "Who wants to go for a hike?" asked Aunt Joan. "There's a new boardwalk that goes all the way around Fossil Lake."

Everyone scrambled for their boots and shoes. "Come with us in our car," Kyle said to Shelley.

"Okay," said Shelley. She climbed into the backseat between Marcus and Kyle.

"I can't wait to get to Fossil Lake," said Marcus. "I want to look for more fossils for my collection."

"Fossil Lake is a conservation area," said Uncle Ray. "No one is allowed to collect fossils there."

Marcus looked disappointed.

"We can look for fossils at Rocky Beach," said Kyle. "It's just down the road from our cottage."

"All right!" Marcus cheered. "I won first prize for my fossils at the hobby fair. I got a blue ribbon, and my picture was in the newspaper." Marcus leaned around Shelley. "Let's go to Rocky Beach tomorrow," he said to Kyle.

Kyle looked at Shelley. "Do you want to come too?"

Shelley could think of several things she would rather do than go fossil hunting. But she was not going to be left out again. "I'll come," she said.

Chapter Five
THE FOSSIL HUNTERS CLUB

Shelley woke early the next morning. She was finishing breakfast when Kyle and Marcus came into the kitchen.

"Guess what, Shelley?" said Kyle. "Marcus and I have a club. Do you want to join?"

"It's called The Fossil Hunters Club," said Marcus. "It was my idea."

"Kyle and I already have a club," said Shelley. "It's called The Beach Club."

"That's a baby name," said Marcus. "The Fossil Hunters Club is much better."

"The Fossil Hunters Club will be fun," said Kyle. "If you join, we'll have three members."

"Okay, I'll join," said Shelley.

"Do you even know what a fossil is?" asked Marcus.

"Of course I do," Shelley declared. "We learned about them at school. You should see the ones my teacher brought in."

"You should see my fossil collection," said Marcus. "I won first prize at the hobby fair last year."

"You already told us that," said Shelley.

Aunt Joan came into the kitchen. "Where are you three off to this morning?" she asked.

"We're going to Rocky Beach," said Marcus.

"To look for fossils," Shelley added.

"Remember the number-one rule," said Aunt Joan.

"No going in the water by ourselves," said Shelley.

Aunt Joan grinned. "Have a good time," she said. "I hope you make some great finds."

"You should see my fossil collection, Mrs. Sutton," said Marcus. "I won first prize at the hobby fair last year."

Shelley rolled her eyes. How many times was she going to hear about Marcus's fossils? "I'm going to play with Topper while you two finish eating," she said. "I'll wait for you outside."

At the sound of her name, Topper scrambled to her feet. Shelley opened the door, and Topper dashed outside.

"Where's your ball?" asked Shelley.

Topper raced off. She was gone a long time.

When Shelley finally called her, Topper rushed out of the bushes.

"Where's your ball?" Shelley asked again.

Topper looked up at Shelley and whimpered.

Shelley crouched down. "Oh, Topper," she said, "have you lost your favorite ball?"

Chapter Six
THAT'S SOME FIND!

"Shelley, where are you?" Kyle shouted.

Shelley stepped out of the bushes. "Topper lost her ball," she said. "I'm helping her look for it."

"Don't worry," said Kyle. "Topper always finds her ball." He headed for the road. "We're going to Rocky Beach now. Are you coming with us?"

"We can help Topper look for her ball when we get back," Marcus called over his shoulder.

Shelley stared after him. Was Marcus actually being nice for a change? She hurried to catch up.

When Marcus saw Rocky Beach, his eyes lit up. "This is a great place to look for fossils!" he said.

"There must be a gazillion rocks on this beach," said Shelley.

Kyle and Marcus didn't answer. They were already busy searching.

Shelley looked too. She found a couple of rocks with squiggly lines on them. She showed them to Kyle. He thought they were neat, so she gave them to him.

After a while, Shelley was bored. She sat down on a large rock. Beyond, the lake sparkled under the bright sun. Waves slapped up against the shore.

Something caught Shelley's eye. It was an old fishing net, washed up on the rocks.

Shelley went to take a closer look. Suddenly her foot skidded. She looked down. Her foot had pushed up a small pile of rocks. Wait. What was that?

Shelley grabbed one of the rocks. It was lumpy and gray. It reminded Shelley of something, but she couldn't think what. But that didn't matter, because on the rock was the perfect imprint of a tiny shell.

Shelley turned the rock over. She gasped. On the other side was an amazing fossil. It looked like a miniature tree with twisted branches. Beside it were two tiny shells that almost looked like leaves.

"Kyle! Marcus! Look what I found," Shelley yelled.

Marcus and Kyle scrambled over to see.

"Wow!" said Kyle. "That's the coolest fossil I've ever seen!"

Marcus stared at the rock in Shelley's hand. "That's coral," he said. "Where did you find it?"

"Right there," said Shelley, pointing to the small pile of rocks.

In a flash, Marcus was on his hands and knees.

Shelley and Kyle searched too. They found a few small pieces of fossilized coral, but nothing compared with the rock Shelley had found.

"Any luck?" a voice called.

Shelley looked up. Dad and Uncle Ray were coming along the road. Topper raced ahead of them.

Shelley ran to meet them. "Look what I found," she whooped.

Uncle Ray examined the rock. "That's some find!" he said.

Dad grinned. "Shelley, that has to be the find of the day!" he declared.

Chapter Seven
A VISIT TO APPLEGATE FARM

Topper jumped up. She sniffed at the fossil rock. Then she licked it.

Kyle laughed. "Topper thinks your fossil rock is cool too," he said.

Marcus kept staring at Shelley's rock. I'll bet he wishes he had found it, she thought.

"It's lunchtime," said Uncle Ray. "This afternoon we're going to Applegate Farm."

"Yay!" Shelley cheered. "I want to see the animals."

"I like the horses best," said Kyle.

"I like the pigs best," said Shelley.

"Yuck!" said Marcus. "Pigs stink."

"The babies don't," said Shelley. "They are my favorite."

Back at the cottage, Shelley showed Aunt Joan and her mom the fossil rock.

"You had better put it in a safe place," said Mom.

"Good idea," said Aunt Joan. "You don't want to lose that one."

Shelley went to her room. Where would be a good place to put the fossil rock?

She spotted her tote bag on the floor beside her bed. It was her favorite bag. It had a little plaid Scottie dog and buttons on it.

Shelley put the fossil rock on her bed and reached for the bag.

Topper came into the room. She saw the fossil rock. She sniffed it and licked it.

"Did you find your ball yet?" Shelley asked. Topper whimpered. She looked sad.

Shelley patted her. She remembered what Marcus had said. "We'll help you look for your ball later," she said. "Don't worry, Topper. We'll find it." Shelley put the fossil rock into her tote bag. She closed the zipper and put the tote bag back on the floor by her bed.

Topper sniffed at the bag.

"My fossil rock will be safe there," Shelley told her. "Let's go and have lunch."

After lunch, Shelley put on her oldest shoes. You never knew what you might step in at Applegate Farm.

Marcus came down the hall. "Look at this, Shelley," he said. He held out a stone. The stone was pearly white with shiny gold flecks all through it. It was one of the prettiest stones Shelley had ever seen.

"I'll trade you," said Marcus. "I'll trade you for your fossil rock."

Shelley shook her head. "No way," she said. "I'm keeping my fossil rock."

Marcus turned and stomped out the door.

Shelley grabbed her jacket and hurried to the car.

They visited all the barns at Applegate Farm. The last barn was the pig barn. In one of the stalls was a huge pig. Against her belly were one, two, three, four...twelve baby piglets! Imagine having twelve babies to look after, Shelley thought.

After visiting the barns, they went into the old farmhouse.

"Shelley, Marcus, come see this," Kyle called from one of the rooms.

Kyle was standing beside a small table. Shelley and Marcus looked over Kyle's shoulder. Under the glass top was a collection of arrowheads.

"Awesome!" said Marcus.

"My teacher brought some arrowheads to school," said Shelley. She remembered touching one. It felt smooth and bumpy at the same time. It was neat to touch something that might be hundreds or even thousands of years old.

Chapter Eight
SOMETHING LOST

The next morning Kyle and Marcus went back to Rocky Beach. Shelley went to town with her mom and Aunt Joan instead.

When she came back, Kyle and Marcus were sitting outside at the picnic table. The table was covered with rocks.

"Did you find anything interesting?" Shelley asked.

"I did," said Marcus. "Look at this." He held out a small rock. It was pointy at one end.

"It's just a pointy rock," said Shelley.

"It is not," Marcus declared. "It's an arrowhead."

Shelley looked closer. It did look like an arrowhead.

Sort of. But it wasn't like the ones at Applegate Farm.

"I'll trade you for your fossil rock," said Marcus.

"No way," said Shelley. "I'm not trading my fossil rock."

Marcus frowned. He snatched up the rock and went inside.

"Marcus really wants your fossil rock," said Kyle.

"That's too bad," said Shelley. "I'm not trading. Not for anything."

After lunch, Kyle and Marcus went off to build a fort. Shelley went swimming in the lake and played beach ball with the rest of the family.

Topper stayed on the shore and ran along the beach barking. Topper wanted to play, but she did not like the water.

When Shelley walked back to the cottage, Topper followed her.

"I'll play fetch with you as soon as I change," said Shelley.

Topper wagged her tail. But there was no gray, lumpy ball in her mouth.

Shelley remembered. "Poor Topper," she said, "is your ball still lost?"

Topper barked. Shelley patted her. "Don't worry," she said. "As soon as I get changed, I'll help you find it."

Although Shelley and Topper searched and searched, they couldn't find the ball anywhere.

Kyle and Marcus came back from building their fort. Soon everyone joined in the search. They found an old shoe, Uncle Ray's missing cap, a rusty toy truck and part of a broken paddle, but they did not find Topper's ball.

"Don't worry," said Uncle Ray. "Topper always finds her ball."

"It will show up sooner or later," said Aunt Joan.

But this time Topper did not find her ball. This time Topper's ball was lost for good.

Chapter Nine
GONE

The next day after lunch, Marcus came into Shelley's room. "Can I see your fossil rock again?" he asked.

"You've already looked at it a gazillion times," said Shelley. She took the rock from her tote bag and handed it to Marcus.

Marcus turned the rock over and over. "Are you sure you don't want to trade?" he asked.

Shelley shook her head. "My fossil rock is the best thing I have ever found," she said. "I'm going to keep it forever."

Marcus gave the fossil rock back to her. Shelley put it into her tote bag and zipped the zipper.

Later, Shelley decided to go for a walk with her dad and Uncle Ray. The weather had turned cool and windy.

"You'll need a sweater," said Dad.

Shelley went inside. As she headed down the hall, she saw Marcus standing in the doorway of her room.

Marcus looked up at Shelley. Then he ducked into Kyle's room and closed the door.

Shelley stared after him. Had Marcus been in her bedroom? What was he doing there?

"Hurry up, Shelley. We're waiting for you," Dad called through the screen door.

Shelley dashed into her room. Everything looked just as she had left it. She grabbed a sweater and ran outside.

When they got back, Shelley went to find Kyle. He was in his bedroom. He was looking at something on the windowsill.

"Come see this," said Kyle. In his hand was a magnifying glass.

Shelley looked over his shoulder. Kyle was looking at a dead fly. The magnifying glass made it look huge. "Oh, yuck! Gross!" Shelley gagged.

"It's not gross," said Kyle. "Flies are cool."

Shelley made a face. "I'd rather look at something else," she said.

"I know," said Kyle, "let's look at your fossil rock."

"I'll get it," said Shelley. "It's in my tote bag."

She went to her room. Her tote bag was on the floor, just where she had left it.

Shelley picked up the bag. Wait a minute. The zipper was open. She had left it closed.

Shelley reached into the bag. Her heart did a quick flip-flop. The bag was empty. Her fossil rock was gone.

Chapter Ten
GUILTY?

Kyle came looking for Shelley. "What's taking you so long?" he asked.

Shelley was searching under the bed. "My fossil rock is gone," she groaned.

Kyle's eyes widened. "Gone?"

"It was in my tote bag." Shelley scrambled to her feet. She grabbed the tote bag and turned it upside down. "It's empty," she declared. "My fossil rock is gone."

"You must have put it somewhere else," said Kyle. "I'll help you look."

Kyle and Shelley searched her room. They looked everywhere, but they did not find the fossil rock.

"Think, Shelley," said Kyle. "You must have put it somewhere else."

Shelley thought. A picture flashed across her mind. Marcus! That afternoon he had been standing right here in her doorway. He must have been in her room.

"I know where my fossil rock is," said Shelley. She raced out of the room. "I'm going to get it back!"

She found Marcus in the den. He was playing a video game.

Shelley stuck out her hand. "Give me back my fossil rock," she demanded.

"What are you talking about?" Marcus snapped. "I don't have your fossil rock."

Kyle came into the den. He sat on the couch. "Did you find it?" he asked.

Shelley clamped her hands on her hips. "No," she said. "I did not find it because Marcus took it."

Marcus jumped to his feet. "I did not take your fossil rock," he declared.

"You were in my room," said Shelley. "Now my fossil rock is gone."

Marcus's face turned as red as a ripe tomato. "I just went into your room to look at it again," he said. "I put it right back in your bag."

"It isn't there now," said Shelley.

Kyle turned to Shelley. "Marcus wouldn't take your rock," he said.

Shelley didn't answer. She glared at Marcus. He looked guilty. Very guilty.

"Don't worry," said Kyle. "We'll find your fossil rock. We'll get everyone to help look for it."

They told Uncle Ray what had happened. "Something mysterious is going on around here," said Uncle Ray. "First Topper loses her ball. Now you lose your fossil rock."

Shelley wanted to say, "I didn't lose my fossil rock. Marcus took it." But she saw Marcus's face. He looked like he was going to cry.

Shelley was sure Marcus had taken her fossil rock. *Almost* sure. But *almost* wasn't good enough. She didn't say anything.

Although everyone joined in the search, they did not find Shelley's fossil rock.

Chapter Eleven
A SURPRISE

After breakfast the next morning, Shelley's mom got out some baskets.

"Who wants to go raspberry picking?" asked Aunt Joan.

"Not me," said Kyle. "I'm going fishing with Dad and Uncle Ken."

"I don't like fishing," said Marcus. "But I like picking berries."

"I pay good berry pickers a dollar a pail," said Aunt Joan.

"All right!" said Marcus.

Mom turned to Shelley. "You'll have to come raspberry picking too," she said. "We can't leave you home alone."

Shelley groaned. She wanted to stay home alone. Then she could really search for her fossil rock. Everywhere. Especially in Marcus's bedroom.

"Can't I stay by myself?" Shelley pleaded. "There are things I want to do here."

"We won't be leaving for an hour or so," said Mom. "Maybe you can get your things done before then. But when we go, I want you to come with us."

Shelley felt restless. She wanted to look for her fossil rock. She went to her room. Topper followed her.

Shelley picked up a book. Topper paced around the room. She was restless too.

"If your ball wasn't lost, we could play fetch," Shelley said to her.

The minute Topper heard "play fetch," her ears perked up. She barked a happy "Woof!" and raced out of the room.

Had Topper found her ball? Shelley hurried after her.

Topper headed for the back porch. She went right to her doggie bed and shoved her nose under the mattress.

When she looked back at Shelley, she had something
in her mouth.

"Topper, you found your ball!" Shelley cheered.

Topper's tail wagged back and forth. She dropped
the object at Shelley's feet.

Shelley picked it up. Her heart jumped, and she
let out a shriek of delight.

Chapter Twelve
FOUND AND LOST

The object in Shelley's hand was gray like Topper's ball. But it wasn't soft like a ball. And it was heavier than a ball.

Marcus came out to the porch. "Your mom said we're ready to go raspberry picking," he said.

"I found my fossil rock!" Shelley yelled. "Topper had it all the time. I'll bet she took it because it looks like her ball."

Topper looked at the rock in Shelley's hand. She whimpered.

Shelley felt bad. "I'm sorry, Topper," she said, "but you can't have my fossil rock to play with."

"I'm glad you found it," said Marcus.

Suddenly, Shelley felt even worse. She had accused Marcus of taking her fossil rock. And she had been wrong. "I...I'm sorry, Marcus," she said. "I really thought you had taken it."

Marcus frowned. "I told you I didn't take it," he said. "You should have believed me." He shrugged. "Anyway, I'm glad you found it."

Shelley gave a small smile. "Actually, Topper found it," she said.

Aunt Joan joined them on the porch. "Are you two ready to go?" she asked.

She saw the rock in Shelley's hand. "You found your fossil rock!" she said.

Shelley told her what had happened.

"So, Topper had it all the time," said Aunt Joan.

Topper barked when she heard her name.

"I think she took it because it looks like her ball," said Shelley.

Marcus patted Topper. "She needs something else

to play with," he said. Topper wiggled and wagged as though she understood.

"You're right," said Aunt Joan. "But right now we're going raspberry picking. Are you two ready?"

"Yes," said Shelley. Now she wanted to go berry picking. But Topper had to stay behind. She watched everyone leaving and whimpered.

"We'll play with you when we get back," said Marcus.

We? Shelley thought. Does Marcus mean him and me?

In the car, Shelley glanced over at Marcus. He looked sad. Was he upset because she thought he had taken her fossil rock? She wanted to say something to him. But what?

Aunt Joan parked near the raspberry patch. As they got out of the car, Marcus turned to Shelley. "It's all my fault," he said.

Shelley looked at him in surprise. "What's your fault?"

51

"That Topper lost her ball," he said. "Remember a couple of days ago? We were playing fetch with her, and I threw the ball really hard. I'll bet that's when it got lost."

"It's not your fault," said Shelley.

"Yes, it is," said Marcus. Without another word he turned and headed for the raspberry patch.

Chapter Thirteen
LUCKY DAY

Shelley took off her hat and fanned herself. She blew a strand of damp hair away from her face.

Her mom shaded her eyes against the bright sun. "It's too hot to keep picking," she said.

"My pail is full anyway," said Shelley.

"So is mine," said Marcus. "And I'm thirsty!"

"We forgot to bring cold drinks," said Aunt Joan. "Let's drive into town and have an ice-cream cone instead."

"Yay!" Shelley cheered.

"Let's go!" said Marcus.

At Dairylicious, they each chose their favorite ice-cream cone. Then they headed for a picnic bench to eat them.

Shelley was about to sit down when she spotted a shiny quarter on the seat. With a whoop, she picked it up.

"Lucky you," said Marcus.

Shelley grinned. This really was her lucky day.

When they finished their ice cream, Aunt Joan gave Shelley and Marcus each a dollar for the raspberries they had picked.

"Now I have a whole dollar and twenty-five cents to spend," said Shelley.

"I have to pick up a couple of things at the grocery store," said Aunt Joan.

"Can I go to Dollar Daze?" asked Marcus. "They're having a sale. There's something special I want to buy."

"Okay," said Aunt Joan. "We'll meet you there."

"Can I go too?" Shelley asked.

"Yes," said her mom, "but be sure you stay together."

Shelley waited for Marcus to protest, but he didn't say anything. He seemed to be lost in thought.

"You can find some really good stuff at Dollar Daze," said Shelley as they started off. "What are you going to buy?"

"It's a secret," said Marcus. "You'll find out later." He had a big grin on his face.

What is Marcus going to buy that makes him so happy? Shelley wondered.

Chapter Fourteen
SOMETHING SPECIAL

"Wait up," called Shelley. Marcus was walking up and down the aisles so fast she could hardly keep up with him.

Shelley stopped. Ahead was a big bin. A sign on the bin said *Everything Half Price*.

She looked up. Marcus was at the other end of the aisle. What was he looking at? Shelley couldn't see. She turned back to the bin.

As Shelley searched through the bin, she found stickers and notebooks and pencils. She found tiny dolls and big earrings. She found party hats and balloons and little stuffed animals. She dug deeper into the bin and pulled out a necklace.

"Oooh," Shelley gasped, holding it up. The necklace was made of woven string. A pretty silver-colored shell hung from the middle.

Shelley held her breath as she looked at the price tag. It was marked down to a dollar. Shelley almost cheered out loud. She had enough money to buy it.

She hurried to catch up with Marcus. "Have you found anything?" she asked.

Marcus showed Shelley a ball. The ball was red and blue and had a white stripe around it.

"Neat ball," said Shelley.

"Topper would like it," said Marcus.

So that was the special something Marcus was looking for! "Topper will love it," said Shelley. "She doesn't have anything to play with since she lost her old ball."

Marcus put the ball back in the bin. "I can't buy it," he said. "The ball costs a dollar ninety-eight. I only have one dollar."

Shelley looked at the bin. It was not marked *Everything Half Price* like the bin she had found her necklace in.

Shelley looked at the necklace. It was pretty. It was special. She thought about Topper. Topper was more special.

"If we put my dollar and your dollar together," Shelley said, "we can buy the ball."

Marcus stared at her. "Really? Wow, Shelley, you're the best!" he said. His hand stopped halfway to the bin. "Uh-oh, we won't have enough for tax."

Shelley pulled the shiny quarter from her pocket. "Yes, we will," she said. "We'll have just enough."

"Not enough for your necklace," said Marcus.

Shelley looked at the necklace. "I don't really need a necklace," she said slowly.

"I have an idea," Marcus said. "I can help you make one. We learned how to weave necklaces in Cubs last year."

"I love making stuff," Shelley exclaimed. "It will be fun to make my own necklace. I'll bet I can even find a real shell to put on it." She grinned. "Let's go buy Topper's ball."

As soon as Marcus and Shelley got home, they showed Topper her new ball. Topper wiggled and wagged. She raced back and forth, barking loudly.

Shelley threw the ball. Topper jumped up and caught it in her mouth.

"Good catch!" Marcus cheered.

Topper ran toward Marcus and dropped the ball at his feet. Shelley and Marcus and Topper played fetch until they were tired.

Afterward, Marcus asked Aunt Joan for some string. He showed Shelley how to weave a necklace.

When Kyle came home, Topper showed off her new ball. Shelley showed off her new necklace. And Kyle showed off the big fish he had caught.

"Let's go to Rocky Beach," said Marcus.

"Maybe I can find a shell for my necklace there," said Shelley.

"Maybe I can find a super fossil rock," said Marcus.

Topper picked up her ball and ran after them.

"Topper wants to come too," said Kyle.

"She can help us look for fossils," said Shelley. "She's good at finding fossil rocks."

"I think Topper should be a member of The Fossil Hunters Club," said Marcus. "All in favor say 'Yay!'"

"Yay!" said Shelley.

"Yay!" said Kyle.

Topper barked. It sounded like she was saying "Yay!" too.

Marilyn Helmer is the author of many children's books, including picturebooks, early readers, novels and retold tales. *The Fossil Hunters* is Marilyn's second book in the Orca Echoes series. Her first is *Sharing Snowy*, published in 2008. Marilyn and her husband live in Fergus, Ontario.